A Note to Parents and Caregivers:

Read-it! Readers are for children who are just starting on the amazing road to reading. These beautiful books support both the acquisition of reading skills and the love of books.

The RED LEVEL presents familiar topics using common words and repeating sentence patterns.
The BLUE LEVEL presents new ideas using a larger vocabulary and varied sentence structure.
The YELLOW LEVEL presents more challenging ideas, a broad vocabulary, and wide variety in sentence structure.

When sharing a book with your child, read in short stretches, pausing often to talk about the pictures. Have your child turn the pages and point to the pictures and familiar words. And be sure to reread favorite stories or parts of stories.

There is no right or wrong way to share books with children. Find time to read with your child and pass on the legacy of literacy.

Adria F. Klein, Ph.D.
Professor Emeritus
California State University
San Bernardino, California

First American edition published in 2003 by
Picture Window Books
5115 Excelsior Boulevard
Suite 232
Minneapolis, MN 55416
1-877-845-8392
www.picturewindowbooks.com

First published in Great Britain by Franklin Watts, 96 Leonard Street, London, EC2A 4XD
Text © Barrie Wade 2001
Illustration © Nicola Evans 2001

Printed in the United States of America.
1 2 3 4 5 6 08 07 06 05 04 03

Library of Congress Cataloging-in-Publication Data
Wade, Barrie.
  The three billy goats gruff / written by Barrie Wade ; illustrated by Nicola Evans.—1st
American ed.
    p. cm. — (Read-it! fairy tale readers)
  Summary: Three clever billy goats outwit a big, ugly troll that lives under the bridge they must
cross on their way up the mountain.
  ISBN 1-4048-0070-0
  [1. Fairy tales. 2. Folklore—Norway.] I. Evans, Nicola, ill. II. Title. III. Series.
  PZ 8.M8038 Th 2003
  398.2'09481'01529648—dc21
  [E]   2002072298

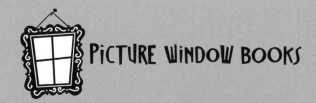

PICTURE WINDOW BOOKS

The Three Billy Goats Gruff

Written by Barrie Wade

Illustrated by Nicola Evans

Reading Advisors:
Adria F. Klein, Ph.D.
Professor Emeritus, California State University
San Bernardino, California

Ruth Thomas
Durham Public Schools
Durham, North Carolina

R. Ernice Bookout
Durham Public Schools
Durham, North Carolina

Picture Window Books
Minneapolis, Minnesota

Once upon a time,
there were three Billy
Goats Gruff.

The three Billy Goats
Gruff were very hungry.

Sweet grass grew in the meadow on the other side of the river,

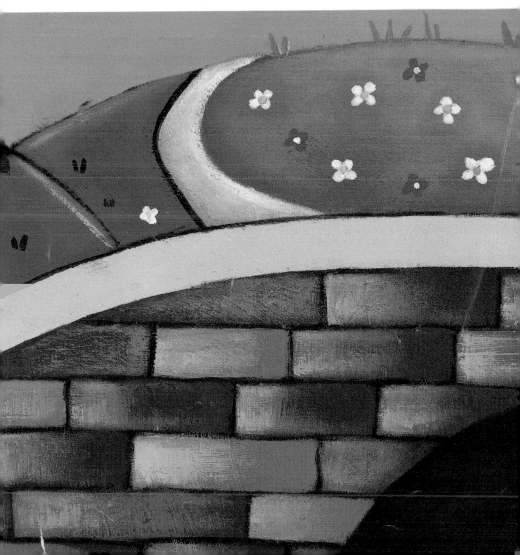

but a wicked old troll
lived under the bridge.

8

The littlest Billy Goat Gruff
clattered onto the bridge.

"Who's that trip-trapping across my bridge?" the troll roared.

"It's only me!" squeaked
the littlest Billy Goat Gruff.

11

"I'm going to eat you up!"
roared the wicked troll.

"But my brother is much fatter than I am," said the littlest Billy Goat.

"Really?" said the troll, and he let the littlest Billy Goat cross his bridge.

Then, the middle-sized Billy Goat clattered onto the bridge.

"Who's that trip-trapping across my bridge?" the troll roared.

"It's only me!" said the middle-sized Billy Goat.

"I'm going to eat you up!"
roared the wicked troll.

"But my brother is even fatter than I am," said the middle-sized Billy Goat.

"Really?" said the troll, and he let the middle-sized Billy Goat cross his bridge.

Then, the biggest Billy Goat clattered onto the bridge.

"Who's that trip-trapping across my bridge?" roared the wicked troll.

"ME!" bellowed the
biggest Billy Goat Gruff.

"I'm going to eat you up!"
roared the wicked troll.

"Oh no you're not!"
the biggest Billy Goat
roared back.

"Oh yes I am!" roared
the troll.

The biggest Billy Goat
Gruff snorted, put down
his head, and charged.

He butted the troll up into
the air, right off the bridge,
and into the river.

The wicked old troll was never seen again.

The three Billy Goats Gruff
ate the sweet grass
in the meadow—

and lived happily
ever after.

Red Level

The Best Snowman, by Margaret Nash 1-4048-0048-4
Bill's Baggy Pants, by Susan Gates 1-4048-0050-6
Cleo and Leo, by Anne Cassidy 1-4048-0049-2
Felix on the Move, by Maeve Friel 1-4048-0055-7
Jasper and Jess, by Anne Cassidy 1-4048-0061-1
The Lazy Scarecrow, by Jillian Powell 1-4048-0062-X
Little Joe's Big Race, by Andy Blackford 1-4048-0063-8
The Little Star, by Deborah Nash 1-4048-0065-4
The Naughty Puppy, by Jillian Powell 1-4048-0067-0
Selfish Sophie, by Damian Kelleher 1-4048-0069-7

Blue Level

The Bossy Rooster, by Margaret Nash 1-4048-0051-4
Jack's Party, by Ann Bryant 1-4048-0060-3
Little Red Riding Hood, by Maggie Moore 1-4048-0064-6
Recycled!, by Jillian Powell 1-4048-0068-9
The Sassy Monkey, by Anne Cassidy 1-4048-0058-1
The Three Little Pigs, by Maggie Moore 1-4048-0071-9

Yellow Level

Cinderella, by Barrie Wade 1-4048-0052-2
The Crying Princess, by Anne Cassidy 1-4048-0053-0
Eight Enormous Elephants, by Penny Dolan 1-4048-0054-9
Freddie's Fears, by Hilary Robinson 1-4048-0056-5
Goldilocks and the Three Bears, by Barrie Wade 1-4048-0057-3
Mary and the Fairy, by Penny Dolan 1-4048-0066-2
Jack and the Beanstalk, by Maggie Moore 1-4048-0059-X
The Three Billy Goats Gruff, by Barrie Wade 1-4048-0070-0